This Little Tiger book belongs to:

_____

_____

_____

for Tim and Emily
with love
~ P.L.

for Aaron
~ P.I.

LITTLE TIGER PRESS
An imprint of Magi Publications
1 The Coda Centre, 189 Munster Road, London SW6 6AW
www.littletigerpress.com

First published in Great Britain 2000
by Little Tiger Press, London.
This edition published 2010

ISBN 978-1-84895-186-0
Printed in China
2 4 6 8 10 9 7 5 3 1

I'll Always Love You

by
Paeony Lewis

illustrated by
Penny Ives

LITTLE TIGER PRESS

One morning Alex woke up early
and ran downstairs to the kitchen.
"I'll make Mom some toast and
honey for breakfast," he said.
"She'll like that."

Alex reached for the honey bowl and . . .

CRASH!

His mom's favorite bowl was
now nine pieces of sticky china.

Alex hadn't *meant* to break it. What would she say?

Alex's mom was doing her morning exercises.
"Hello, Alex," she said. "Did I hear something break?"
"Mom, will you only love me if I'm good?" asked Alex.

"I'll always love you," said his mom, and she smiled.

"Even when I've done something that *isn't* good?" asked Alex.

"I'll still love you," said his mom. "Honest."

"What if I have a pillow fight with Joey Bear and
all the feathers burst out? Will you still love me?"
"I'll always love you. Though you must
pick up all the feathers."

"What if I spill my new paints on Baby
Pog and she turns green, red and blue?
Will you still love me?"
"I'll always love you. Though you
will have to give her a bath."

"What if I forget to close the fridge
door and Baby Pog pulls everything out?
Will you still love me?"
"I'll always love you. Though there
won't be any food for dinner."

"What if I pour Grandma Bear's lumpy oatmeal
all over my head? Will you still love me?"
"I'll always love you. Though you will have to
eat another bowl of oatmeal. Now, why are you
being such a silly bear this morning?"

For a few moments Alex didn't say anything.
Then he whispered, "What if I break your
favorite honey bowl? Will you still love me?"
"You know I'll always love you,"
said his mom. "Come on, Alex,
it must be time for breakfast."

And off they went to the kitchen.

"Oh no!" cried his mom
when she saw the pieces
of sticky china.
"That was my favorite
bowl, Alex."

"Sorry," said Alex. Two tears ran down
his face. "You said you would still
love me. I love *you*."

"Of course I love you,"
said Alex's mom,
hugging him.

"Hey, I've got an idea!" shouted
Alex, wriggling from her arms.
"What is it?" she asked.
"It's a surprise," Alex said
and he ran off to his bedroom.

He looked in his toy box . . .

He looked in his closet . . .

and he looked under his table.

At last he found what
he wanted.

He got out his new paints, poured
some water into a jelly jar, and
swirled his paintbrush around.

A little while later, Alex came downstairs again.
"Here you are, Mom," he said. "But be careful,
the paint's still wet."
"I'll be *very* careful," said his mom, smiling.
"Because this is going to be my new
favorite honey bowl!"

More fantastic reads from Little Tiger Press!

For information regarding any of the above titles or for our catalog, please contact us:
Little Tiger Press, 1 The Coda Centre, 189 Munster Road, London SW6 6AW, UK
Tel: +44 (0)20 7385 6333 • Fax: +44 (0)20 7385 7333 E-mail: info@littletiger.co.uk • www.littletigerpress.com